AROUND AUSTRALIA with

This book belongs to

Harry

RILLA ALEXANDER

This book would not have been possible without the visionary support of Paulina de Laveaux and Tahlia Anderson; and the entire Thames & Hudson team.

My endless gratitude to the Jacky Winter team: Bianca Bramham, Fushia O'Hara, Li Liang Johnson, Sam Raphael, Sarah Ewing, Sarah Laurens and Shena Jamieson who went above and beyond to bring this project to life.

We would be nothing without the incredibly talented artists who we have the privilege to represent and work with every day; and who truly made this book what it is. A particularly big thanks to Dave Foster for his original cover design and lettering, and Rachael Kendrick for writing the introduction.

This book is dedicated to Winifred.

— Jeremy Wortsman, The Jacky Winter Group

First published in Australia in 2014
by Thames & Hudson Australia Pty Ltd
11 Central Boulevard Portside Business Park
Port Melbourne Victoria 3207
ABN: 72 004 751 964

www.thameshudson.com.au

Around Australia with Jacky Winter © Thames & Hudson Australia Pty Ltd

17 16 15 14   5 4 3 2 1

The moral right of the illustrators has been asserted.

All rights reserved. No part of this publication may be reproduced or transmitted in any form or by any means, electronic or mechanical, including photocopy, recording or any other information storage or retrieval system, without prior permission in writing from the publisher.

Any copy of this book issued by the publisher is sold subject to the condition that it shall not by way of trade or otherwise be lent, resold, hired out or otherwise circulated without the publisher's prior consent in any form or binding or cover other than that in which it is published and without a similar condition including these words being imposed on a subsequent purchaser.

ISBN: 978 050050 047 7

National Library of Australia Cataloguing-in-Publication entry

    Jacky Winter Group, illustrator.
    Around Australia with Jacky Winter/The Jacky Winter Group (selected illustrators).
    9780500500477
    Coloring books--Australia.
    Drawing books.
    Australia--Pictorial works--Juvenile literature.
    Australia--Juvenile literature.
919.4

Editing: Nan McNab
Design: Pounce Creative
Cover Art: Dave Foster
Inside Cover Art: Marc Martin
Printed and bound in China by 1010 Printing

AROUND AUSTRALIA WITH JACKY WINTER

 Thames & Hudson

ARTISTS

 RILLA ALEXANDER
 PAULE KÖNYE
 JAMES GULLIVER HANCOCK
 EMI UEOKA
 MIKE JACOBSEN
 KAT CHADWICK
 JEREMY LEY

 GRACE LEE
 JAMES FOSDIKE
 MARCELA RESTREPO
 EIRIAN CHAPMAN
 ANDREA INNOCENT
 BENJAMIN CONSTANTINE
 TRAVIS PRICE

 KARAN SINGH
 FORGE & MORROW
 JASON SOLO
 SNIP GREEN
 MICHAEL WELDON
 BEN SANDERS
 ROSS MURRAY

 ADRIAN CLIFFORD
 MADELEINE STAMER
 FLEUR HARRIS
 CAT MACINNES
 FIONA LEE
 KELLY THOMPSON
 CLEMENS HABICHT

 JANE REISEGER
 BEN ASHTON-BELL
 SONIA KRETSCHMAR
 JULIAN FROST
 BECI ORPIN
 CHRISTOPHER NIELSEN
 MATT HUYNH

 MIMI LEUNG
 MARC MARTIN
 TOMMY DOYLE
 GEMMA O'BRIEN
 SOPHIE BLACKHALL-CAIN
 RUDI DE WET
 LILLY PIRI

If you like what you see go to **www.jackywinter.com/all-artists** for full artist portfolios and bios

HELLO NEW FRIEND!

I'm so happy you picked up this book.
Can't wait to spend some time together
and get to know each other. You're probably wondering who made this book and what their favourite colour[1] is and where they like to go on holidays[2] and what their favourite sandwich filling[3] is. Read on to find out the answers.

Who made this book? Well The Jacky Winter Group did. They're like a biker gang, but they make pictures rather than ride bikes. There are lots and lots and lots of them – so many that only 76 out of over 100 were able to help put this book together.

How did they start? Well, one day, many, many, many, many, many years ago, when dinosaurs played Connect 4 with cavemen, there was a group of friends who teamed up. They had two important things in common: they loved to make pictures and they loved Australia.

So back in 2007 they said: *'We don't just want to make pictures for ourselves all alone in our bedrooms. We want to make pictures for lots and lots of people! We want to make pictures for buses and billboards, magazines and newspapers, posters and placards and pamphlets, movie screens and TV screens and computer screens and iPad screens and phone screens, wherever and whenever, and goshdarnit, we're going to do it together!'*

As you know, every team needs a name if they're going to make it big. This group of friends decided to name themselves after me – Jacky Winter.

Who's Jacky Winter, you ask? Am I a person? An object? An animal? Vegetable? Mineral? Am I bigger than a breadbox? Am I standing right behind you? Well, let me introduce myself! I am Jacky Winter. I am a native robin. Some folks call me 'Postboy' or 'Brown Flycatcher' or even 'Peter-Peter', because I like to hang out in the forest calling, 'Peter! Peter! Peter! Peter!' Some people say that if you say 'Peter! Peter!' five times I'll appear and give you a high five. Go on and try it right now. It doesn't matter where you are, I'll wait for you.

Some people say I look like a ping-pong ball with grey-brown feathers on top, white feathers on my tummy, and a perky little beak. I reckon I look like a handsome and friendly ping-pong ball.

But enough about me: you're probably wondering what's coming up next, right? Well there are all kinds of things to do – you'll solve puzzles, start collections and play games, but best of all you'll make lots and lots and lots of pictures and you'll start by making one of me. Turn the page and let's get on our way!

[1] All of them
[2] The beach
[3] Cheese and Vegemite

FEDERATION SQUARE, IN THE HEART OF MELBOURNE, IS A GREAT MEETING PLACE FULL OF ART AND CULTURE. BUT A FEW THINGS HAVE POPPED UP THAT DON'T BELONG HERE.

COLOUR IN YOUR FAVOURITE THINGS.

ARTIST
JAMES GULLIVER HANCOCK

THE AUSTRALIA DAY REGATTA IS ON AT SYDNEY HARBOUR BUT SOME SNEAKY PIRATES ARE TRYING TO RUIN THE RACE! CAN YOU SPOT THEM?

ARTIST
MIKE JACOBSEN

The roof of the Sydney Opera House was designed to look like the sails of a ship on the harbour.

 A WAVE

 A PINEAPPLE

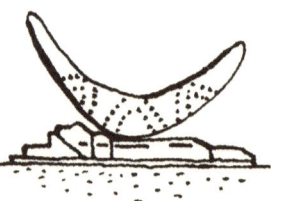 A BOOMERANG

 A FLOWER

DESIGN A NEW ROOF FOR THE OPERA HOUSE.

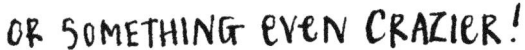

OR SOMETHING EVEN CRAZIER!

ARTIST
KAT
CHADWICK

DRAW YOUR OWN TERRACE HOUSE.

ARTIST
MARCELA RESTREPO

ARTIST
EIRIAN CHAPMAN

YOU'RE SHOPPING AT SALAMANCA MARKET IN HOBART.
CAN YOU FIND THESE ITEMS?

○ strawberries   ○ a loaf of bread   ○ an anchor   ○ a woollen beanie   ○ lollipops

ARTIST
ANDREA INNOCENT

ARTIST
TRAVIS PRICE

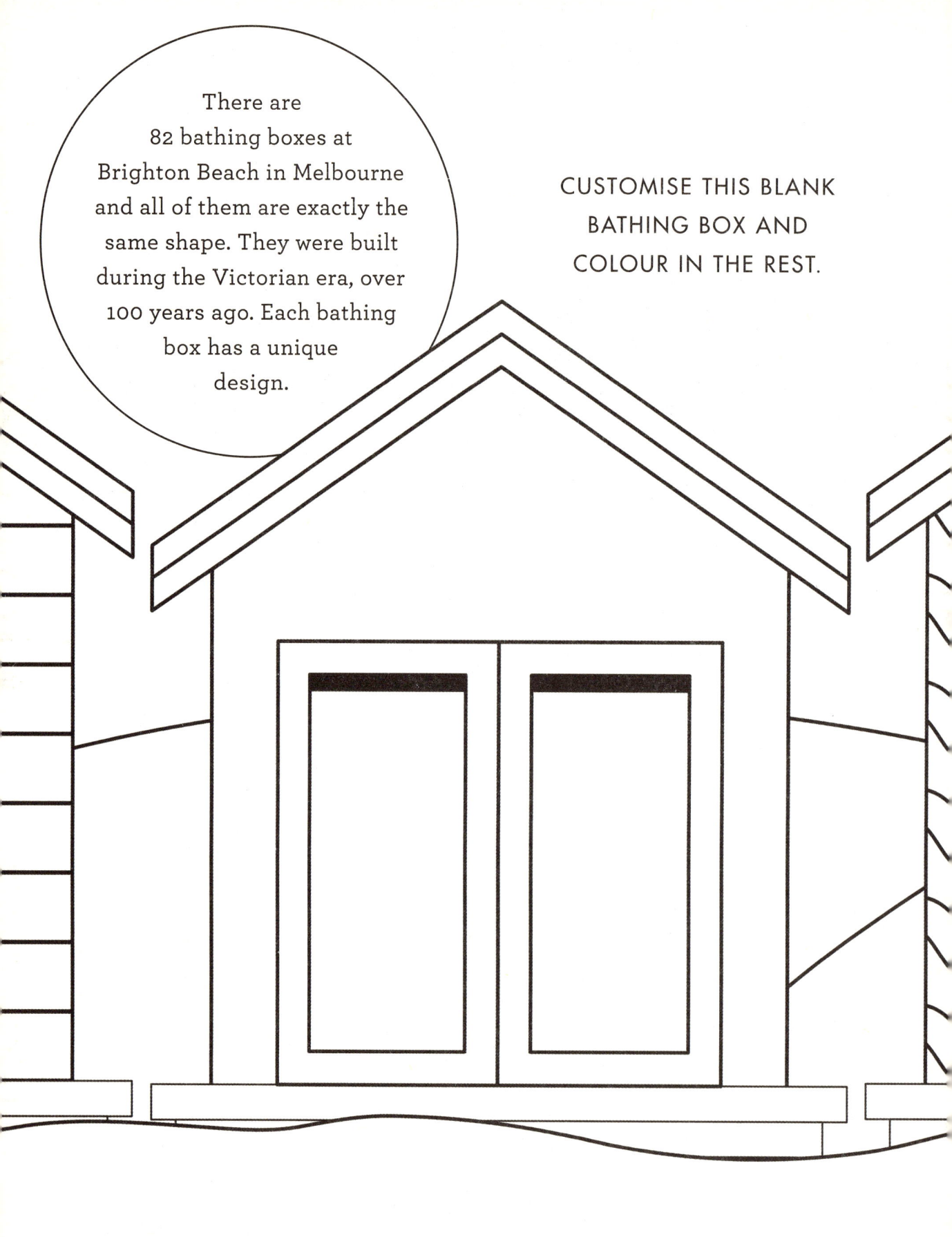

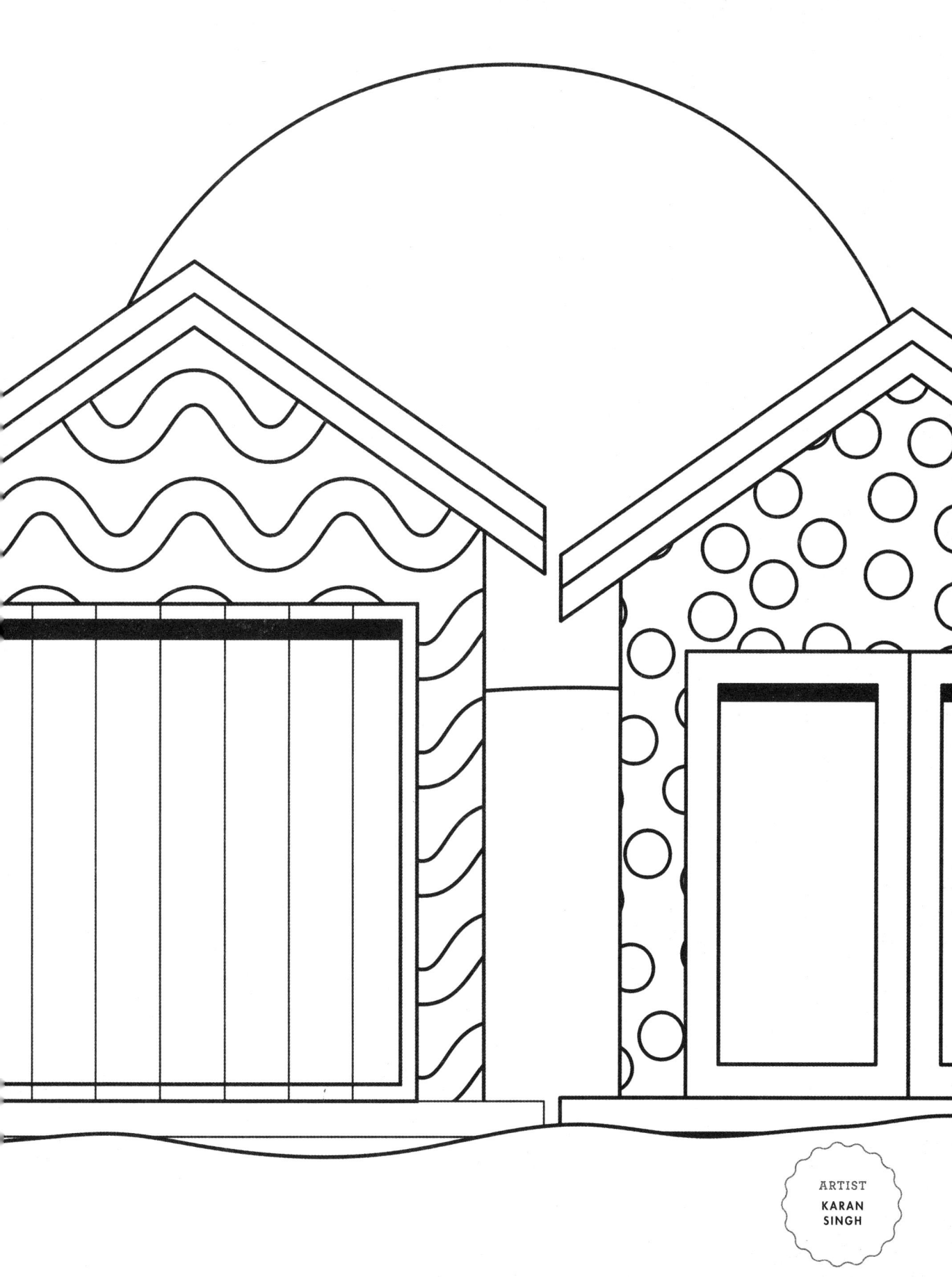

THERE'S A SANDCASTLE COMPETITION ON THE BEACH.
DRAW YOUR BEST SANDCASTLE HERE!

ARTIST
FORGE &
MORROW

ARTIST
JASON SOLO

WHAT DOESN'T BELONG IN THIS ROCK POOL?

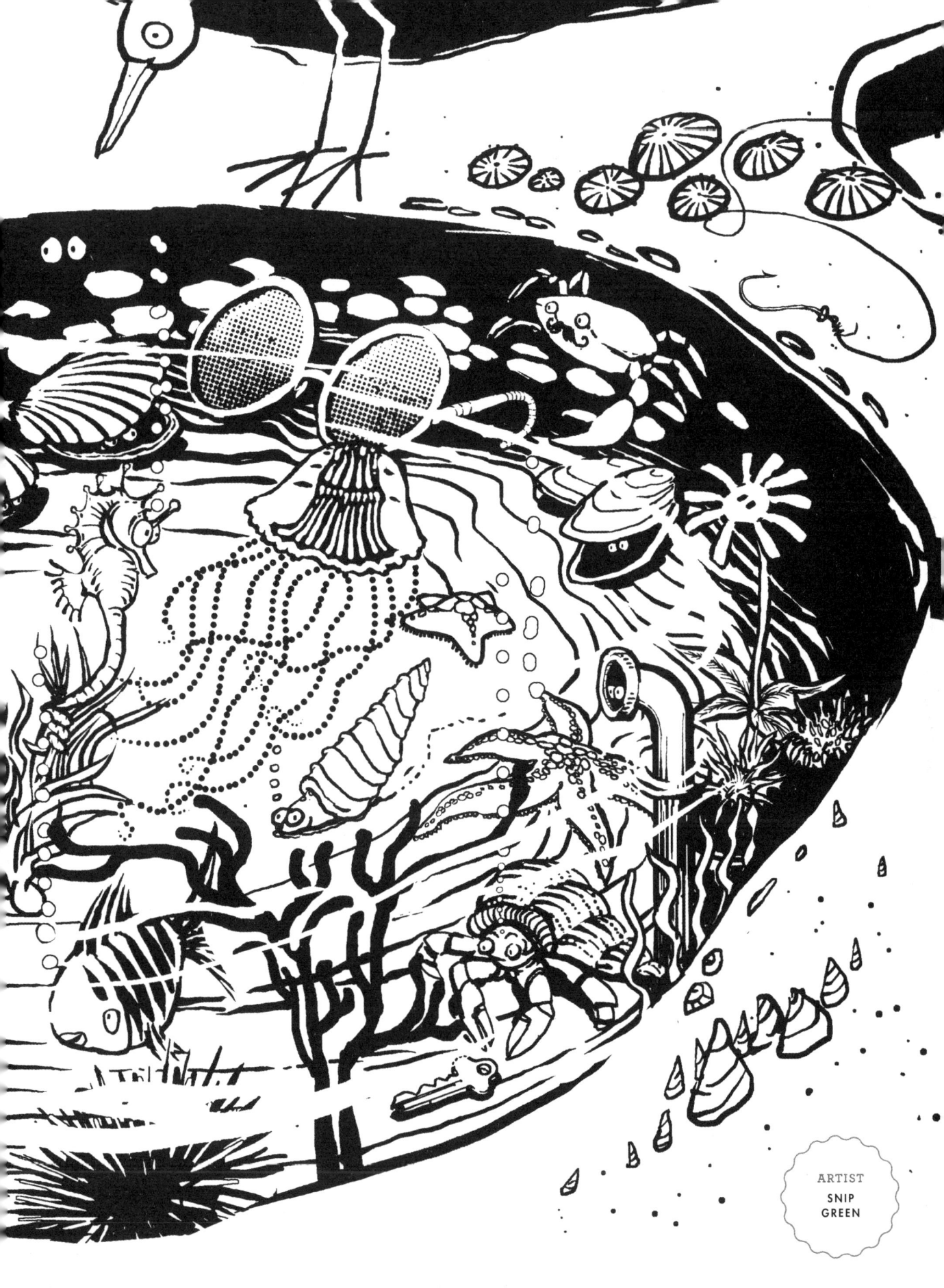

ARTIST
SNIP
GREEN

ARTIST
MICHAEL WELDON

WARM tropical pool

WHICH WATER SLIDE LEADS TO THE WARM POOL?

HELP!

FREEZING cold pool

ARTIST
BEN SANDERS

ARTIST
MADELEINE STAMER

Great white sharks are at the top of the food chain which is probably because they have around 300 teeth! Unlike us, if a shark loses a tooth, a tooth from the row behind fills the gap.

THIS SHARK HAS LOST NEARLY ALL HIS TEETH.
CAN YOU DRAW IN SOME REPLACEMENTS?

ARTIST
FLEUR HARRIS

THESE TWO OUTBACK SCENES ARE NOT QUITE THE SAME.

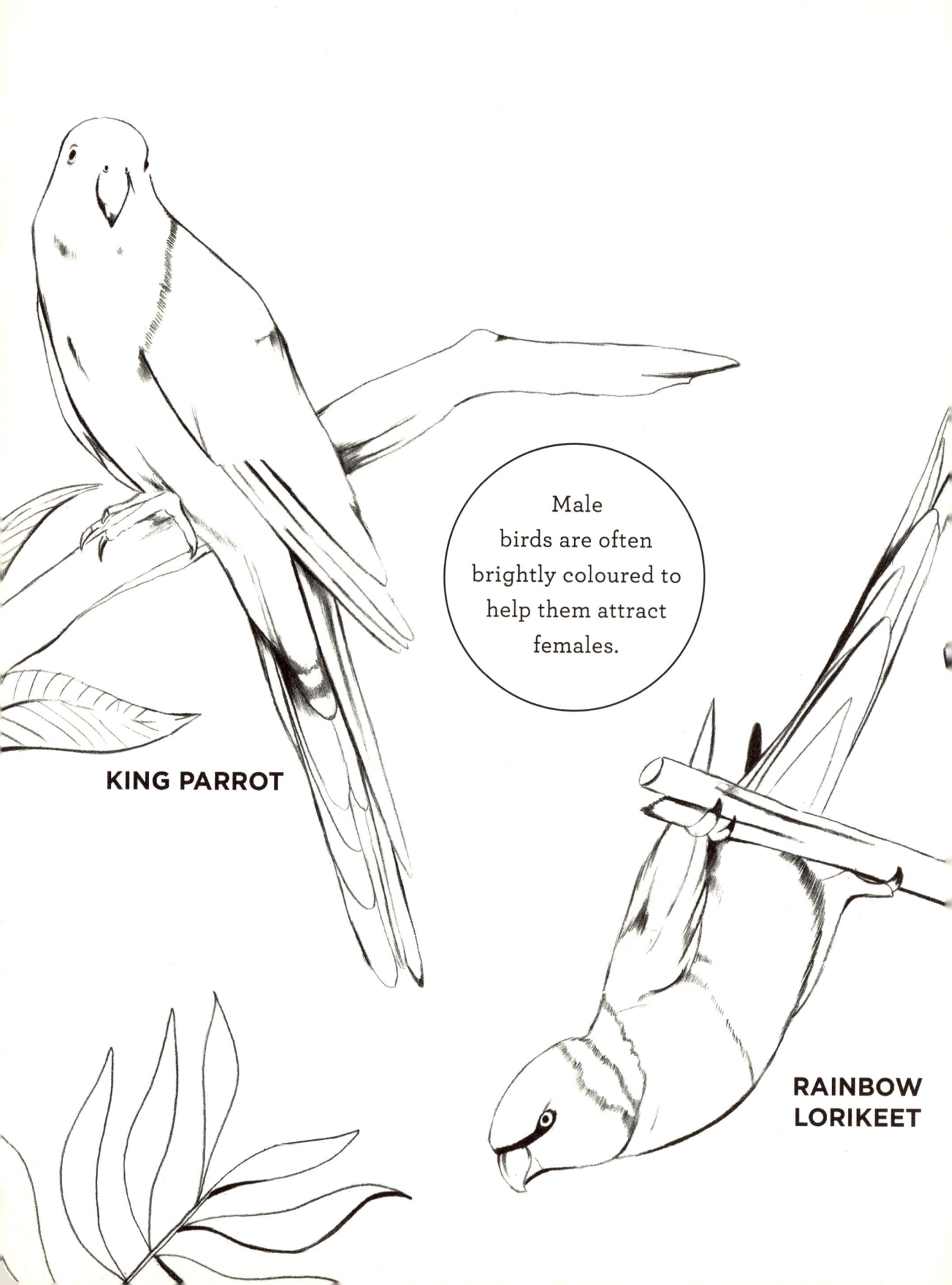

Male birds are often brightly coloured to help them attract females.

KING PARROT

RAINBOW LORIKEET

COLLECT AS MANY DIFFERENT TYPES OF LEAVES AS YOU CAN.
ARRANGE THEM IN THE SHAPE OF ANIMALS
AND GLUE THEM DOWN.

ARTIST
CLEMENS
HABICHT

FLOWER PRESSING

1

Collect some flowers
from your garden or local park.

2

Arrange them between several
sheets of paper towel.

3

Put a folded newspaper on top,
then a few big heavy books on top of that and
leave the flowers to press for a few days.

MAKE A PRETTY PATTERN WITH
YOUR FLOWERS AND STICK THEM
ON THE OPPOSITE PAGE.

DRAW THE MISSING BEAKS AND BILLS FOR THESE ANIMALS.

NOW DRAW THE ANIMALS THAT BELONG
TO THESE BEAKS AND BILLS.

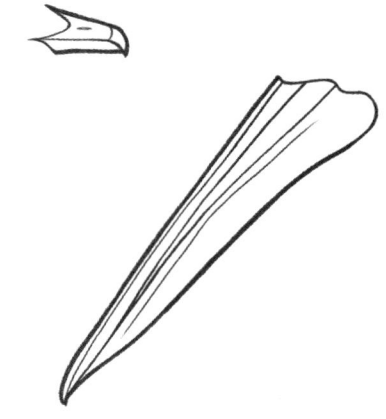

ARTIST
BEN
ASHTON-
BELL

HOW ARE THE RAT AND THE QUOKKA DIFFERENT?

When the Dutch first saw quokkas on Rottnest Island in Western Australia, they thought they were rats!

ARTIST
SONIA KRETSCHMAR

ARTIST
JULIAN FROST

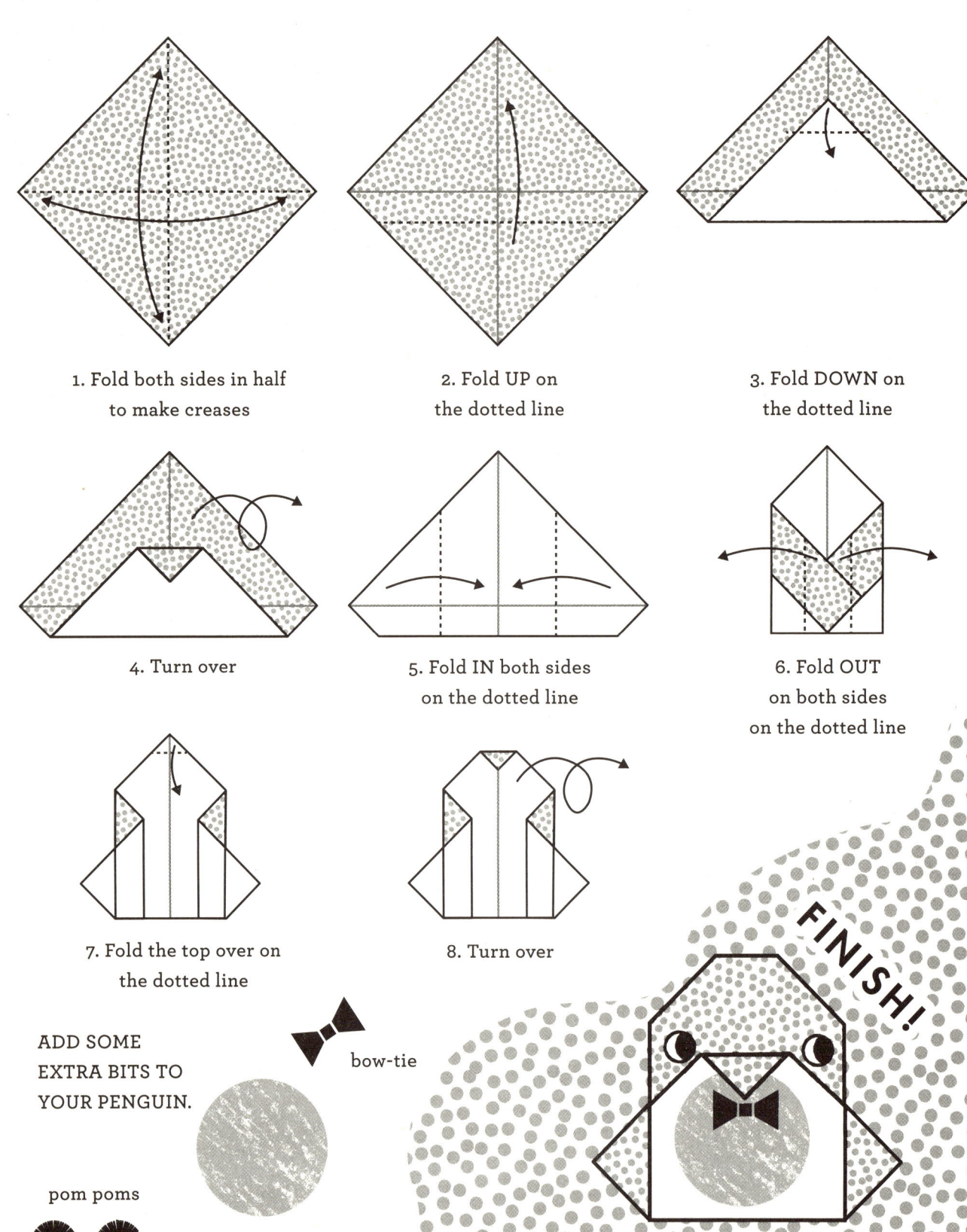

Australia was once populated by lots of different megafauna like giant wallabies, diprotodons and marsupial lions.

ARTIST
MATT HUYNH

CONNECT THE DOTS TO REVEAL THE BIGGEST BIRD IN AUSTRALIA!

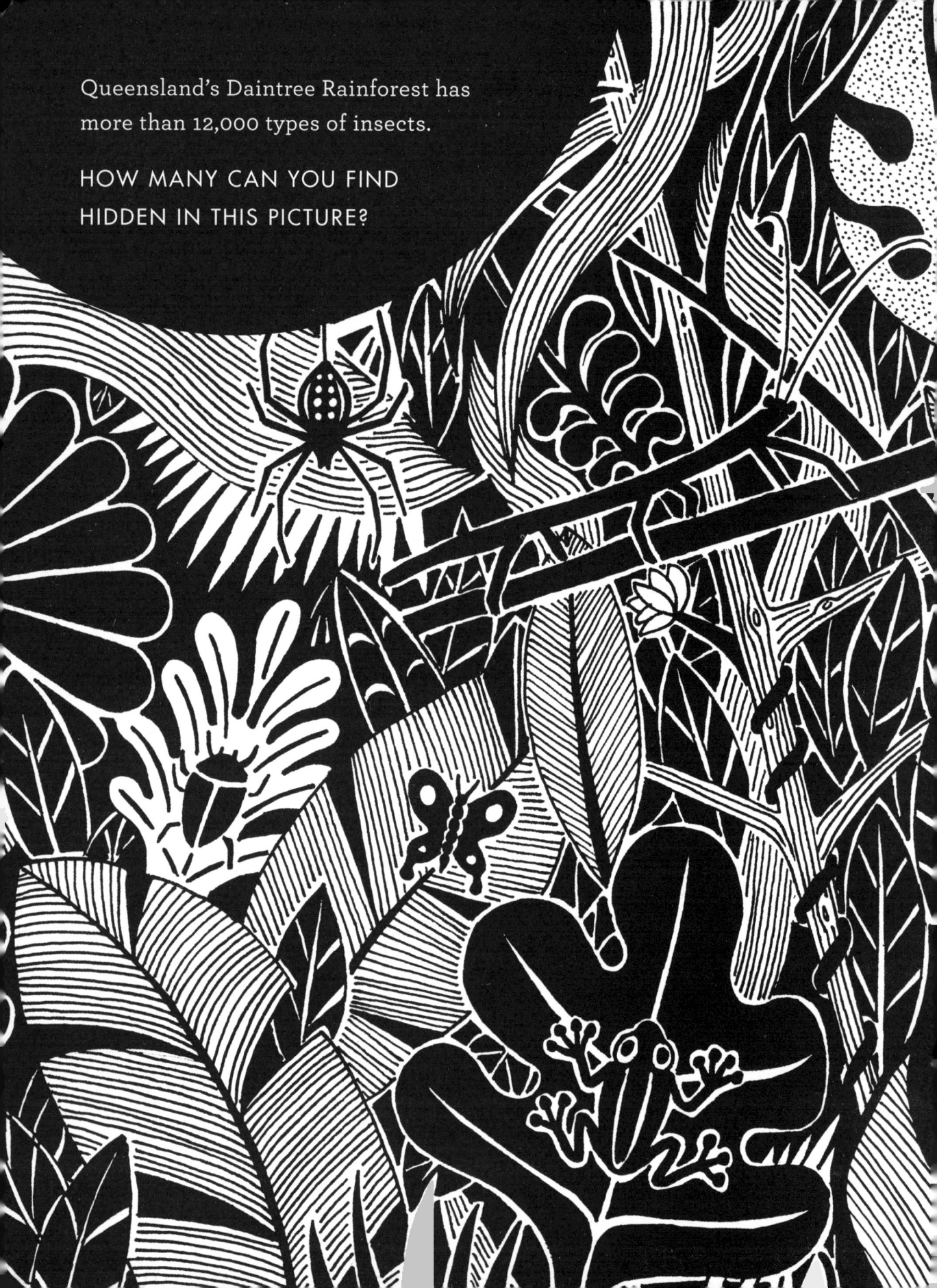

ARTIST
MARC MARTIN

CAN YOU REDRAW THE PICTURE, THE RIGHT WAY UP?

ARTIST
TOMMY
DOYLE

ARTIST
SOPHIE BLACKHALL-CAIN

Wabbyn was an Aboriginal guessing game played by the Injibandi people of Western Australia. Often it was played around the campfire after a long day of hunting.

HERE ARE SOME CLUES TO START YOUR OWN GAME.

I'M OVER ___ YEARS. I AM A SACRED SITE ___ PEOPLE. NO EUROPEANS ___ 1873. 2.5 KM OF MY ___ BULK ___ AROUND 250,000 PEOPLE EACH YEAR. I'M TALLER ___ I'M ORANGE AND RED. CALL ME ___ AYERS ROCK.

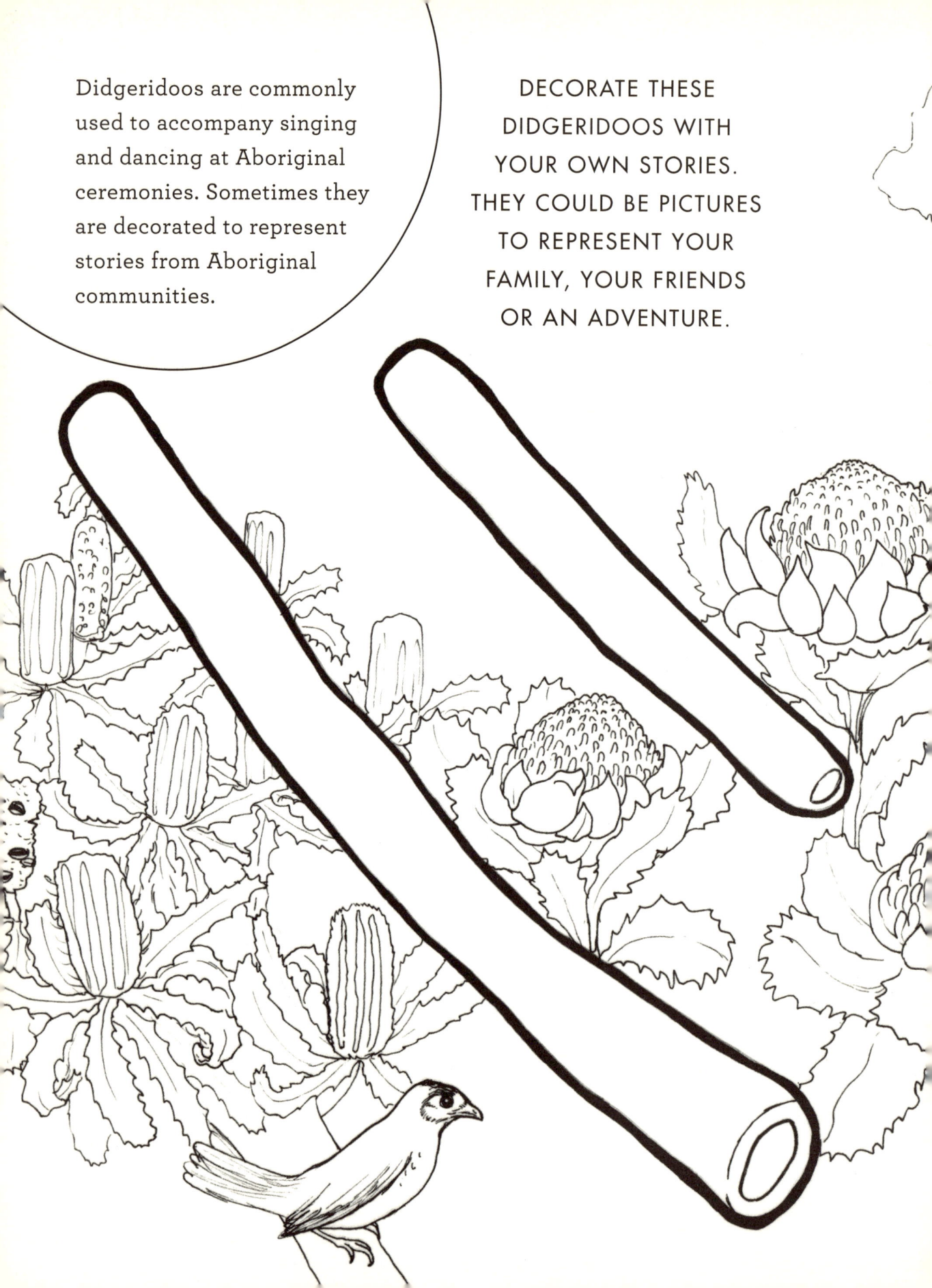

Didgeridoos are commonly used to accompany singing and dancing at Aboriginal ceremonies. Sometimes they are decorated to represent stories from Aboriginal communities.

DECORATE THESE DIDGERIDOOS WITH YOUR OWN STORIES. THEY COULD BE PICTURES TO REPRESENT YOUR FAMILY, YOUR FRIENDS OR AN ADVENTURE.

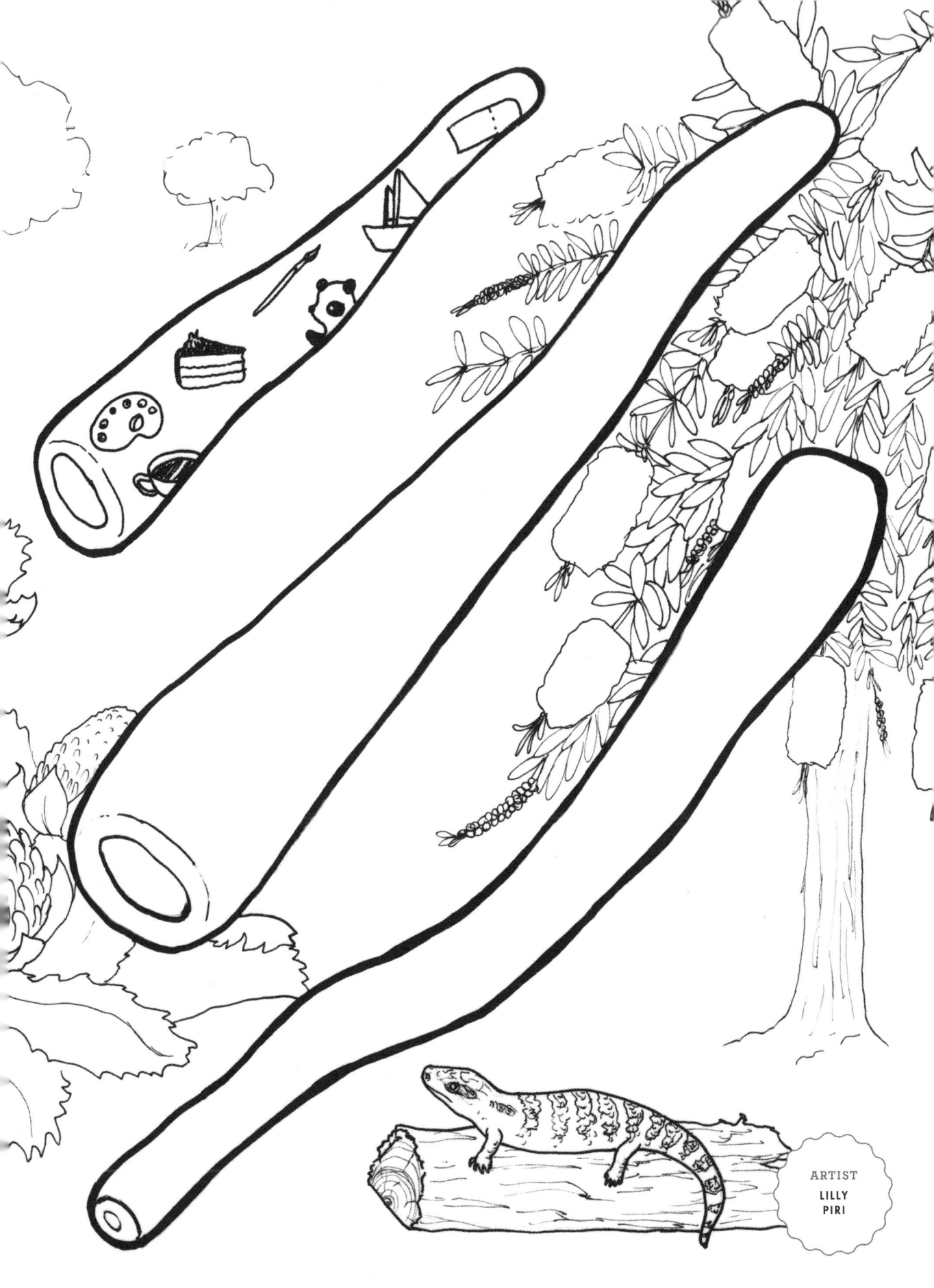

ARTIST
LILLY PIRI

DESIGN SOME JEWELLERY TO SHOW OFF THESE GORGEOUS DIAMONDS. COLOUR THEM IN PRETTY SHADES OF PINK.

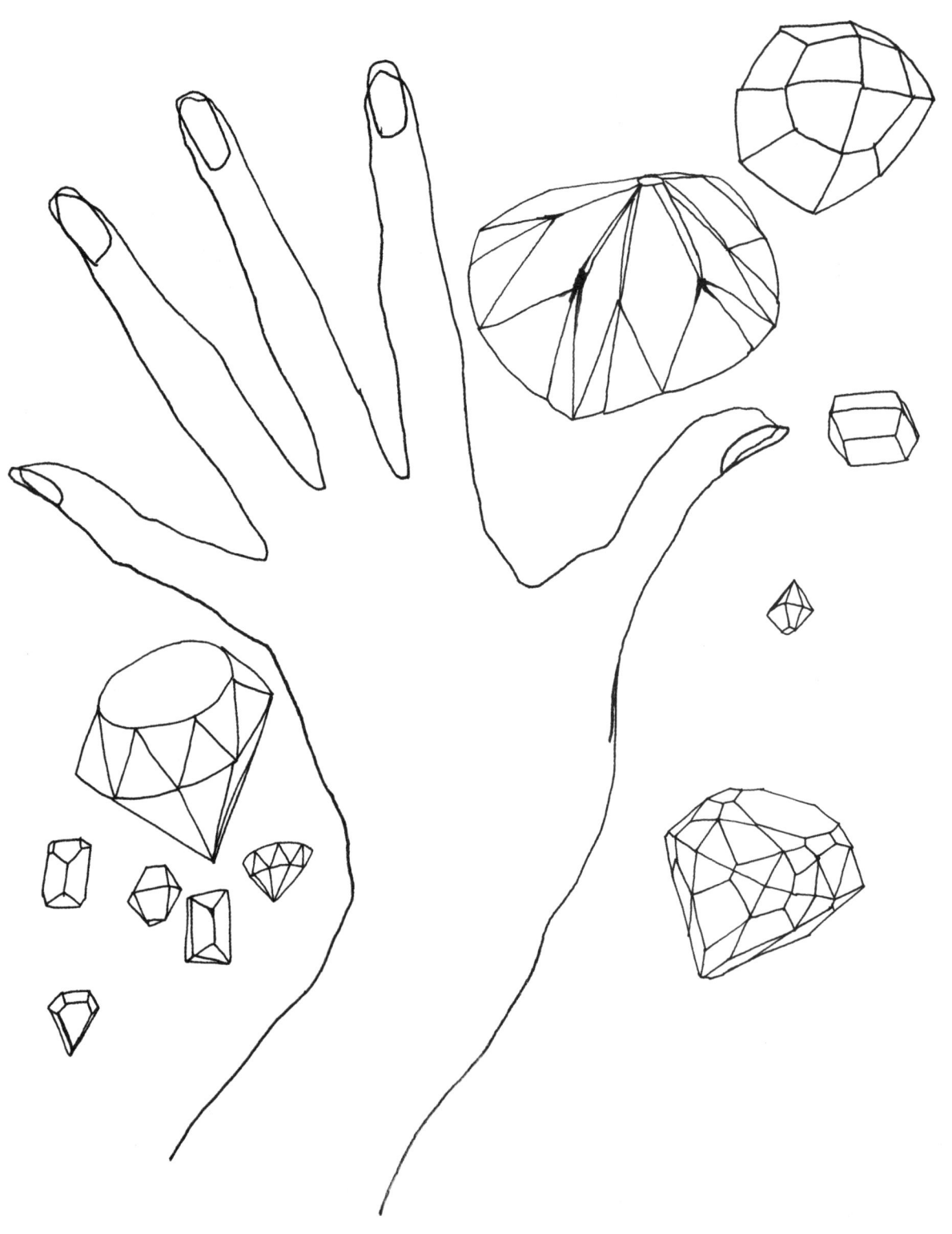

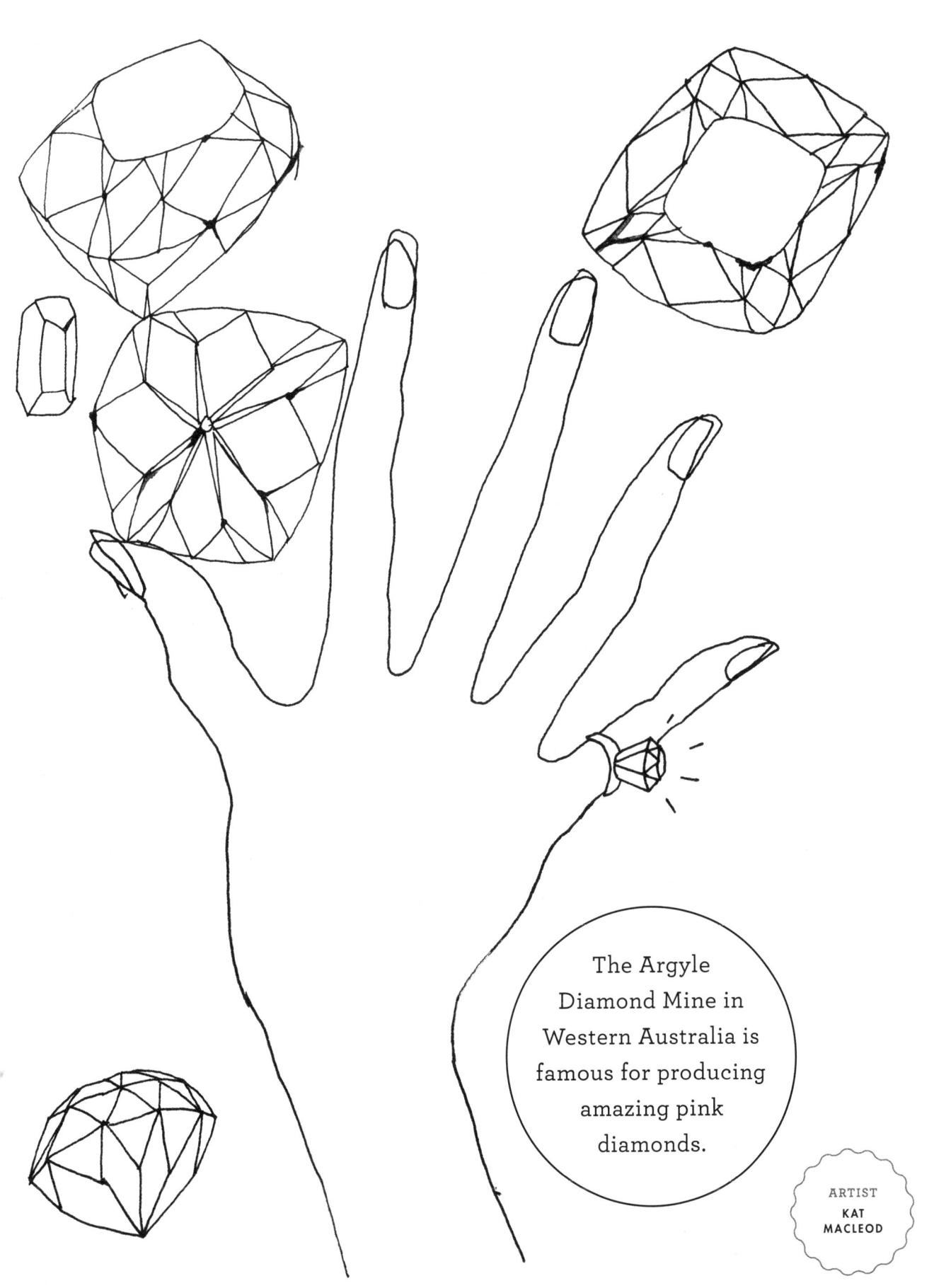

COOBER PEDY IN SOUTH AUSTRALIA IS KNOWN FOR OPAL MINING. COMPLETE THE MAZE TO FIND THE STASH OF OPALS.

AT PARKES OBSERVATORY, THE RADIO TELESCOPE HAS PICKED UP A MESSAGE FROM MARS BUT IT'S IN MARTIAN. HELP THE ASTRONOMERS DECODE IT.

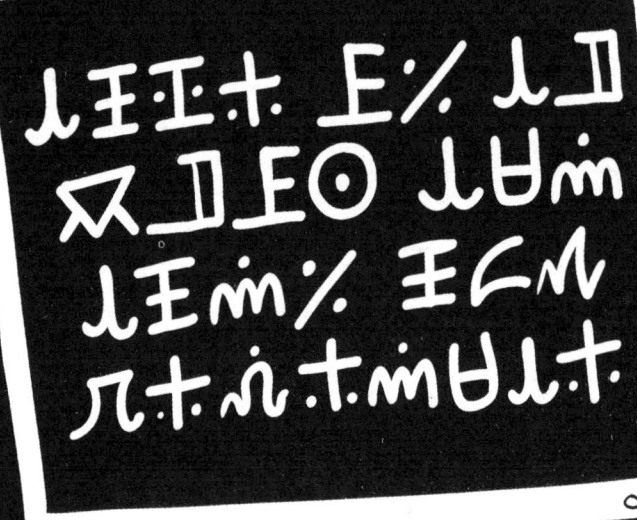

___ ___ __ __

___ ___ ___ ___ ___ ___ ___ ___

___ ___ ___ ___

ARTIST
TIM MOLLOY

WHAT WOULD YOU TAKE CAMPING?
DRAW YOUR ULTIMATE CAMP SITE.

ARTIST
TOM
HUTTON

ARTIST
LUKE LUCAS

ARTIST
OSLO DAVIS

You'll commonly find a returning boomerang in tourist shops. Unlike the hunting tool, which is differently shaped, it is more of a toy. Curved and very light, it is designed to fly back towards you when you throw it!

MAKE YOUR OWN RETURNING BOOMERANG WITH FOUR ICY POLE STICKS.

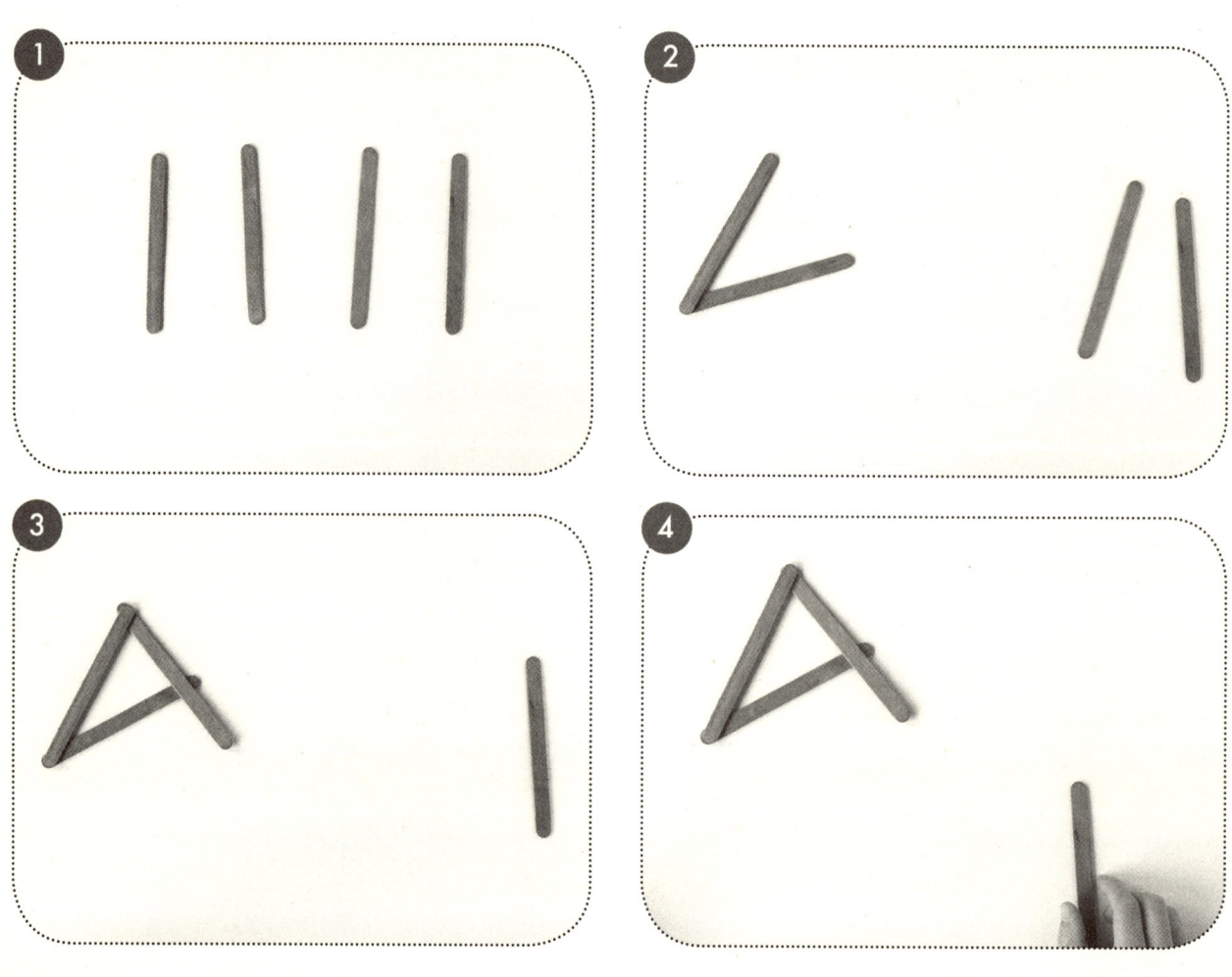

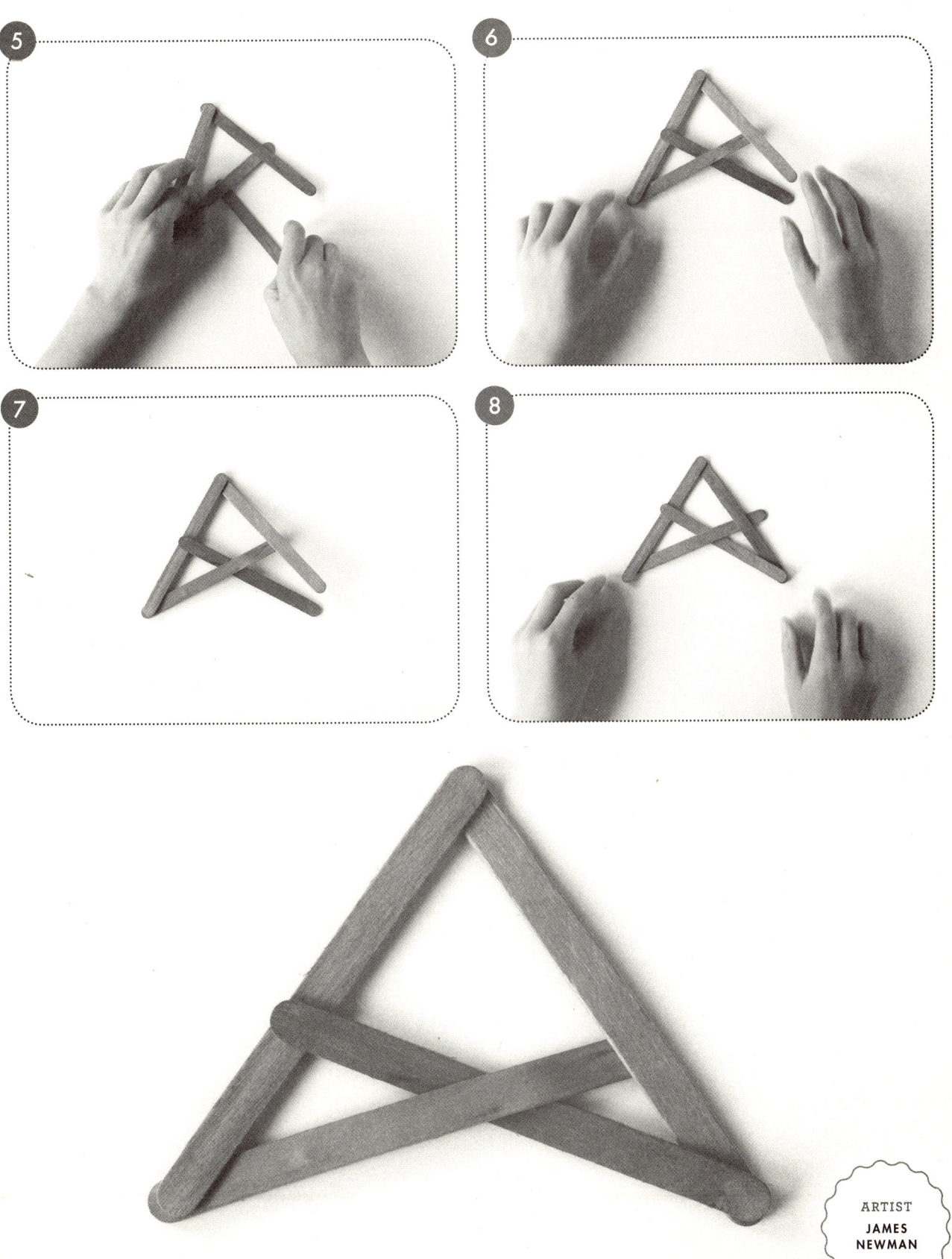

ARTIST
JAMES NEWMAN

FILL THE SUITCASE WITH THINGS YOU'D TAKE WITH YOU ON HOLIDAY.

ARTIST
MEGAN
HESS

PLAY TRAVEL BINGO ON YOUR NEXT CAR TRIP. SEE HOW LONG IT TAKES YOU TO FILL IN THE BINGO SHEET OR PLAY AGAINST A FRIEND – WHOEVER SPOTS ALL THE ITEMS FIRST WINS!

TRAVEL Bingo

1. Volkswagen Beetle
2. Boat
3. Bridge
4. Stop Sign
5. Sun
6. Motorcycle
7. Cow
8. Surfboard
9. Picnic Area
10. Petrol Station
11. Satellite Dish
12. Cloud
13. Caravan
14. Helicopter
15. Poo
16. Traffic Cone
17. Skateboard
18. Tent
19. Fish
20. Wattle
21. Road Kill
22. Bee
23. Kangaroo Sign
24. Bicycle
25. Ute
26. Bus
27. Dog
28. Aeroplane
29. Spider
30. Suitcase
31. Sheep
32. Windmill
33. Gum Tree
34. 100kph Sign
35. The Southern Cross
36. Semitrailer
37. Thongs
38. Magpie
39. Traffic Light
40. Moon

ARTIST
SAM BEVINGTON

DRAW A BIG THING OF YOUR OWN.
IT COULD BE YOUR FAVOURITE FOOD, SPORT
OR PERHAPS SOMETHING YOU'VE JUST MADE UP.

ARTIST
NIGEL
BUCHANAN

WRITE A POSTCARD TO A FRIEND OVERSEAS TELLING THEM ABOUT THE BEST THINGS TO SEE AND DO IN AUSTRALIA!

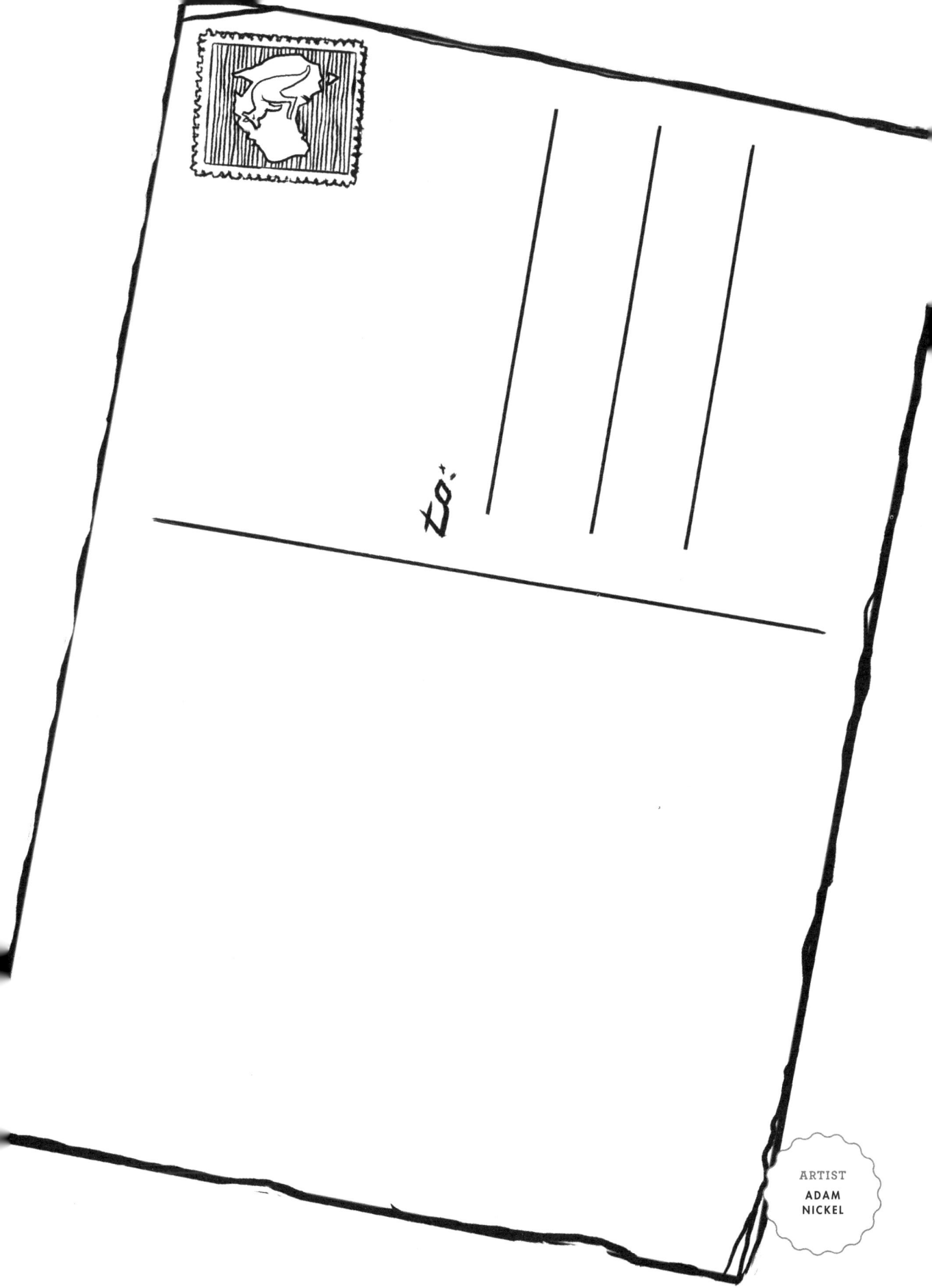

Flags use symbols to represent a land and its people. Important flags in Australia include the Australian flag, the Aboriginal flag and the Torres Strait Islander flag.

- UNION JACK, THE BRITISH FLAG — RED, WHITE AND BLUE
- SOUTHERN CROSS — WHITE
- FEDERATION STAR — WHITE
- THE ABORIGINAL PEOPLE — BLACK
- THE SUN — YELLOW
- THE EARTH — RED
- SYMBOL OF PEACE — WHITE
- THE SEA — BLUE
- THE LAND — GREEN

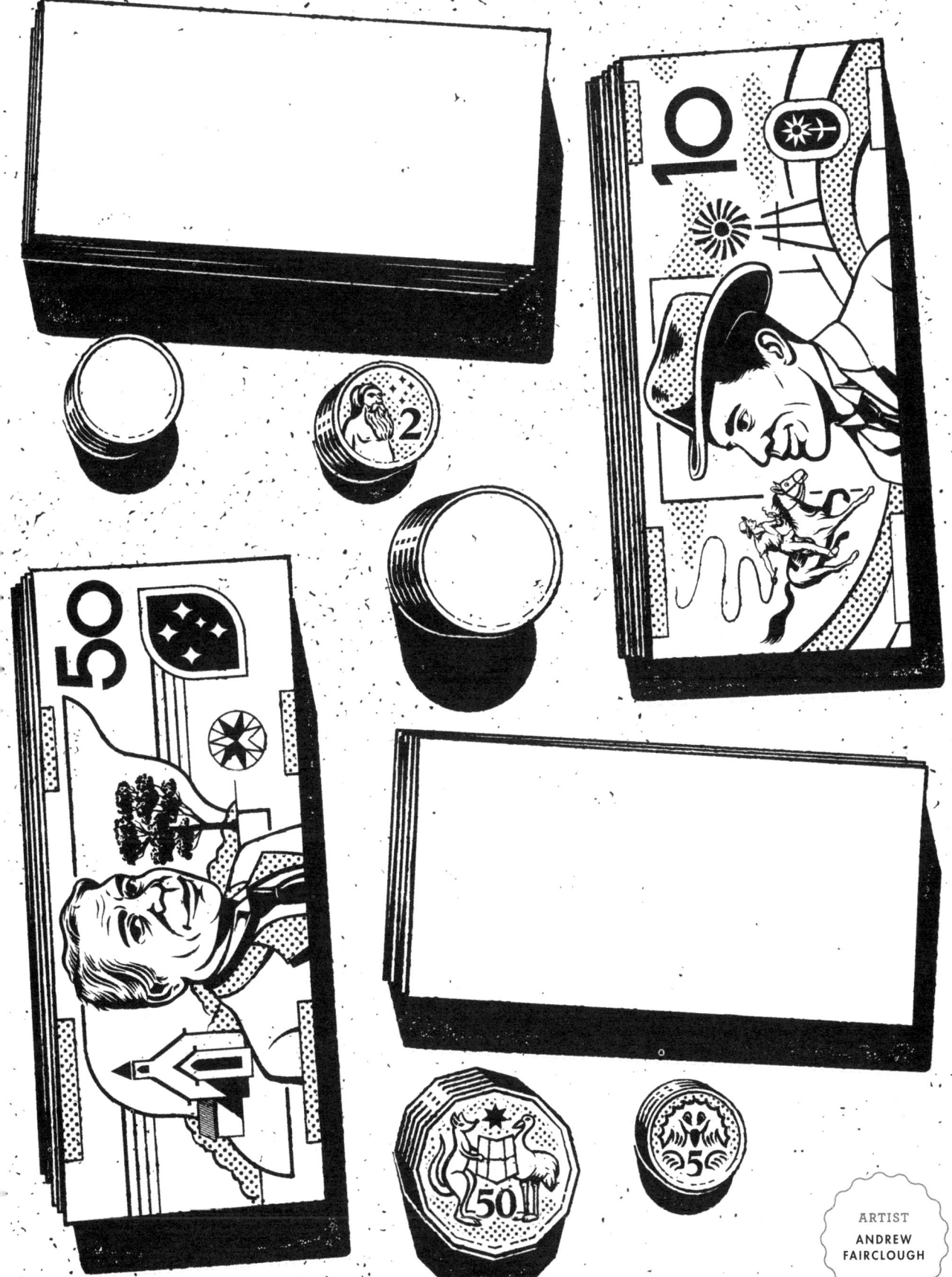

ARTIST
ANDREW FAIRCLOUGH

COME UP WITH YOUR OWN STAMP DESIGNS.

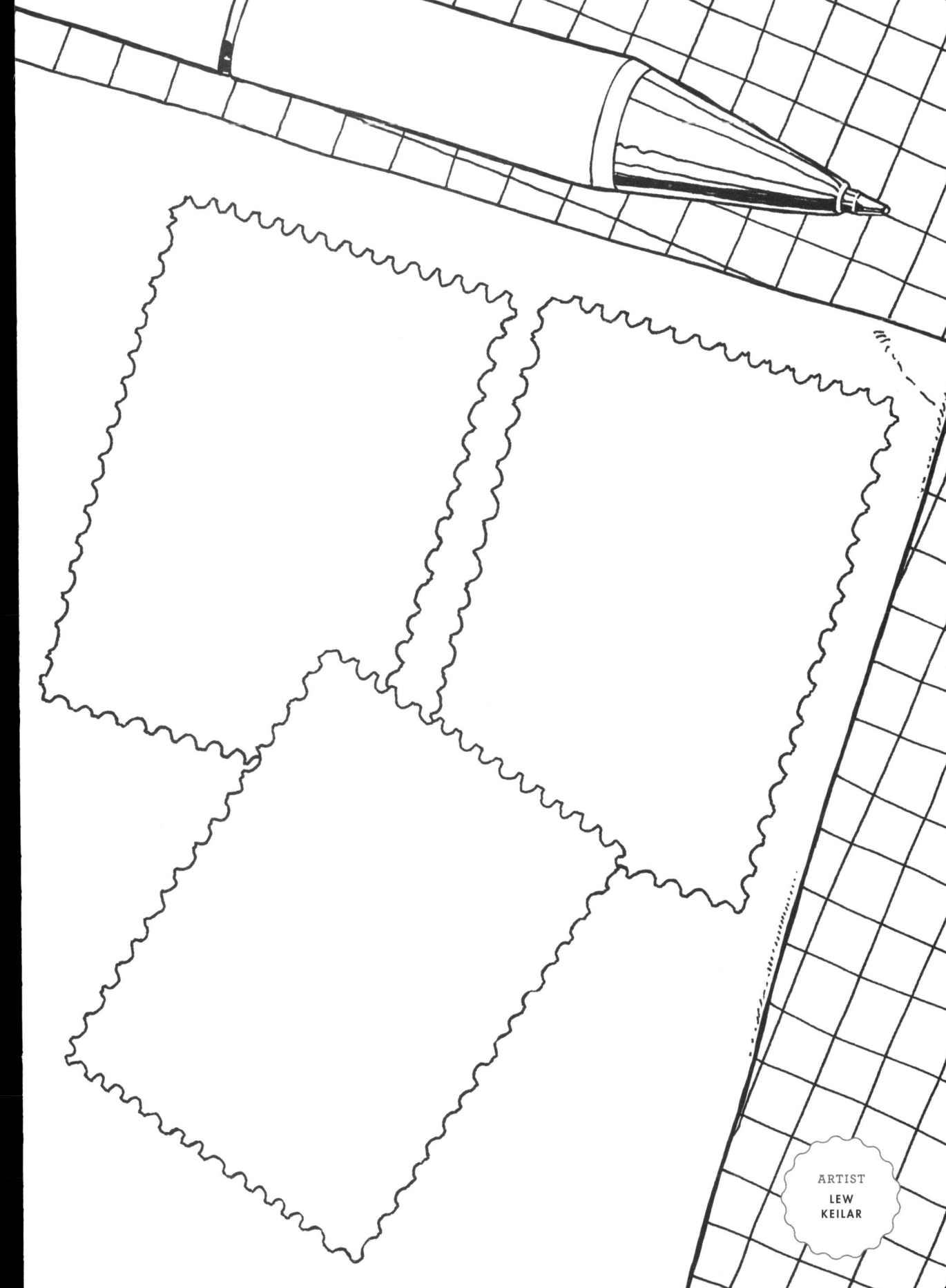

HAVE A GO AT WRITING YOUR NAME
USING THIS AUSTRALIANA ALPHABET.

AUSTRALIA

ARTIST
DAVE
FOSTER

CUSTOMISE THESE SOUVENIRS.

ARTIST
A IT
THEY I

ARTIST
DANNY COHEN

GO TO ONE OF AUSTRALIA'S ART GALLERIES
AND PLAY ART BINGO!

ART BINGO

CITYSCAPE		PORTRAIT
ARTWORK / ARTIST		ARTWORK / ARTIST
	ANIMAL ARTWORK / ARTIST	
AUSTRALIAN		LANDSCAPE
ARTWORK / ARTIST		ARTWORK / ARTIST

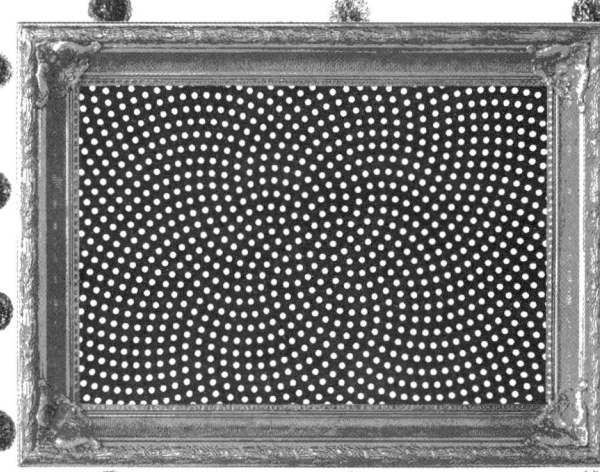

ARTIST
HEATH KILLEN

WHILE I WAS AT THE MUSEUM
I ALSO SAW _____
_____
_____

I ENJOYED THE MUSEUM BECAUSE
_____
_____
_____
_____

SOMETHING I LEARNT AT THE
MUSEUM WAS _____
_____
_____

ARTIST
ALLISON
COLPOYS

ARTIST
DIEGO
PATINO

NEXT TIME YOU VISIT AN ART GALLERY,
CHOOSE YOUR FAVOURITE WORK AND SKETCH IT.

WRITE A DESCRIPTION OF THE ARTWORK
AND WHAT YOU LIKED MOST ABOUT IT.

ARTIST
BOBBY HAIQALSYAH

Australians and New Zealanders love to argue about who invented the Pavlova. But everyone agrees it was made in honour of Russian ballerina Anna Pavlova.

HERE ARE SOME CLASSIC AUSSIE ICE-CREAMS. COLOUR THEM IN!

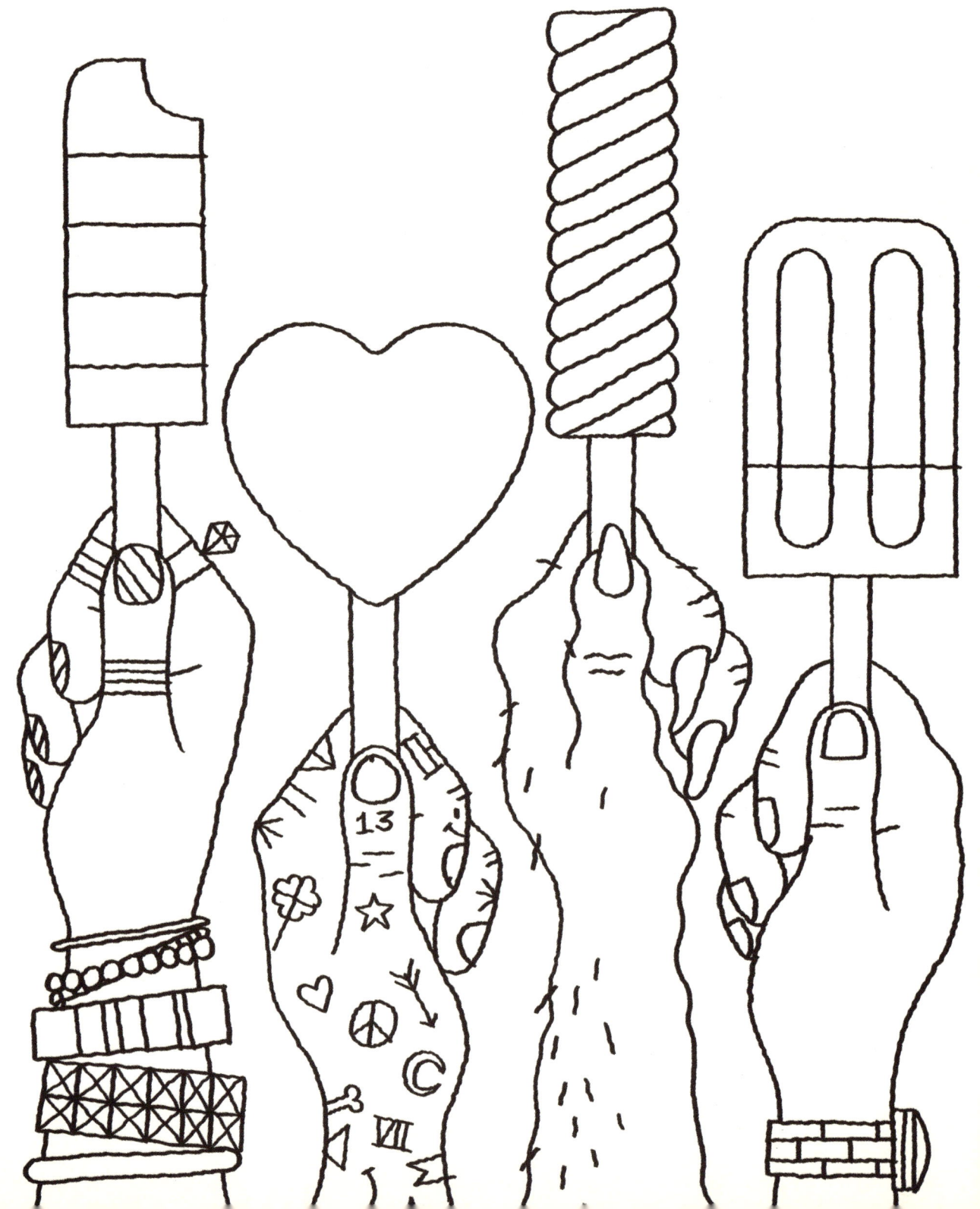

NOW DRAW YOUR ULTIMATE ICE-CREAM TREAT.

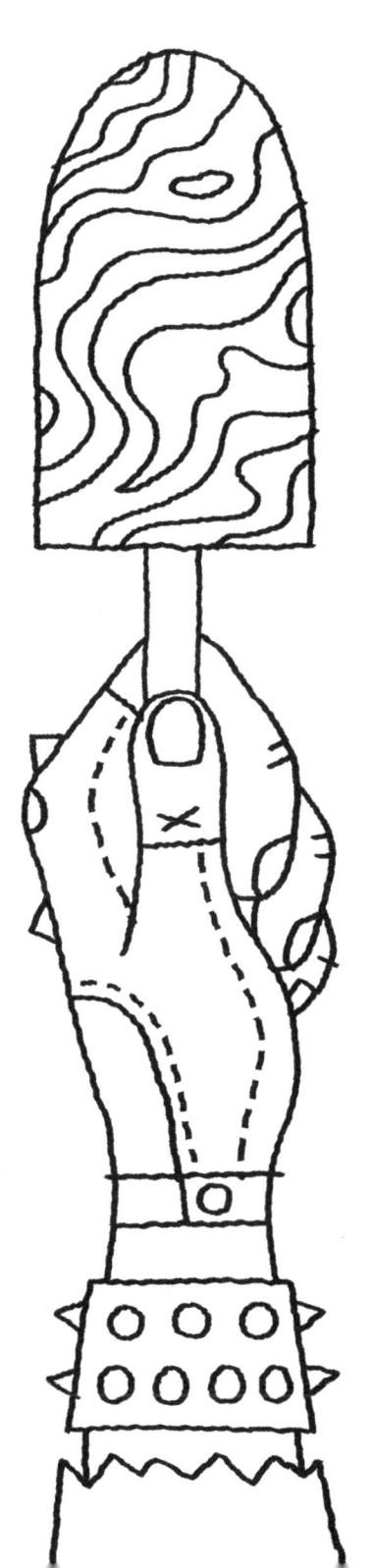
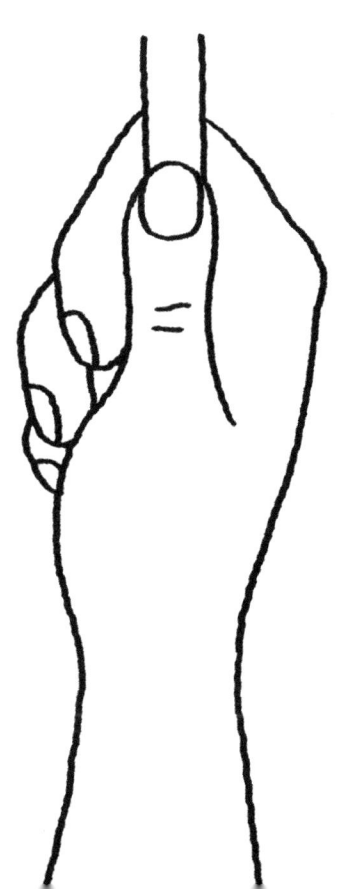

ARTIST
LACHLAN CONN

Marngrook means 'game ball' in some Victorian Aboriginal languages. Many people believe Australian rules football is based on this game Aboriginal people played with a possum-skin ball.

HOW TO PLAY

One player kicks the ball into the air and everyone else must attempt to catch it.

CONGRATULATIONS – YOU'RE THE OWNER OF A NEW AFL TEAM! WHAT WILL YOUR TEAM BE CALLED? COME UP WITH A NAME AND A DESIGN FOR YOUR TEAM'S GUERNSEY.

ARTIST
SHARP BROTHERS

ARTIST
ROMEO VARGA

THESE BILLYCARTS ARE ALMOST READY TO RACE. ADD SOME FINAL RACING DETAILS TO GIVE THEM THAT EXTRA OOMPH!

ARTIST
STUART MCLACHLAN

CREATE A COLLAGE USING THE MEMENTOS YOU'VE COLLECTED ON YOUR TRAVELS.

ARTIST
LAUREN BAMFORD

MAKE A TIME CAPSULE!

ALL ABOUT YOU

How Old Are You?

. . . .

What's Your Favourite Movie?

. . . .

What Do You Want To Be When You Grow Up?

. . . .

What's Your Favourite Song?

. . . .

Do You Have A Pet?

. . . .

What's Your Favourite Food?

. . . .

What's Your Hobby?

. . . .

ARTIST
EMMA
LEONARD